Don't the Let Flies In

for
Mary Stewart
Enjoy
Megan Joppa

Don't Let the Flies In

Edith's Stories

Maryann Hopper

Alpharetta, GA

ISBN: 978-1-61005-600-7

10 9 8 7 6 5 4 3 2   0 4 0 9 1 5

Printed in the United States of America

♾ This paper meets the requirements of ANSI/NISO Z39.48-1992 (Permanence of Paper)

*For Drea Firewalker and my many
women friends along my writing path.*

"Mourning is the downside of love."

- Kenny T.

Contents

Acknowledgments

Many thanks go to all my writing teachers, my fellow writers at Callanwolde, at UU, and at Womonwrites for their inspiration and creative suggestions, and to my sisters at Unity and our Crone Council for their constant encouragement.

Cooling Off

*L*ord, I don't know what I was thinking when I said yes to my friend Ruby this afternoon. But my husband, Kenny T, had stirred me up, and I wanted to make a believer out of him.

*

Yesterday, I had just finished frying up some little peach pies when Kenny T held the screen door open long enough to let three flies in. They buzzed into the window over the sink. My flailing arms scattered them for a minute before they settled right on top of some of the pies I had laid out to cool on the sink counter.

"How many times have I told you not to lollygag at the door when I'm cooking?"

"Flies won't hurt 'em 'cause they'll be gone before any poison sets in," he mouthed off and scooped up a pie in each hand, taking off the end of one with a sloppy bite, the peach filling dripping all over his hand and a gooey plop landing on my clean linoleum floor.

"They're good enough to sell at Angela's bake shop. Angie would let you, said so before."

"I made them 'cause they're your favorite."

I reached with one finger to wipe off the dab of mushy filling on his cheek and popped it in my mouth. He cut his eyes to give me that little-boy twinkly glance and nodded.

"Awww, I know it. Just wanting to share with the unlucky folks that don't have a fine cook in their home—plus, you're always looking to make money, Edith."

"I made good money at the last Spring Festival. Eat what you want, but don't go boxing up any of my pies to share with those gals at the mill when you go to work tomorrow." I folded my arms and pressed my back against the sink, showing him I meant business.

"They'd buy 'em, too. You're off from school all summer, got plenty of time to bake more." He licked the peach filling from his hand and shoved the rest of that pie between his thin lips, not raising his curly head toward me again.

"That's not the point, and you know it." I wiped the stream settling around my neck with a dishtowel, tossing it hard into the closest ladder-back chair. Early menopause and a hot kitchen do not mix with a smart-alecy husband. "I've made three dozen, not for sharing, and I'm done with baking this week."

*

My friend Ruby and I have speculated that he didn't always keep his britches zipped away from home. One day at the County Clerk's office where she worked, she'd over-heard Mary Claire on the phone talking to him about "a little joy ride." He'd always been a flirt so I just hoped that's all he did, but sometimes he prickled my skin the way he talked about those mill gals.

I started writing down in a spiral notebook what worries me lately. Would he really miss me if I were gone? We've been married for a long time, married in our thirties. I was in no hurry, since my first true love was dead. Dating was wearing out Kenny T and costing him plenty, so he finally made a decision. He never minded my weight. We've had a lot of good years, even without children.

*

Being on school break from cooking in the cafeteria meant I could sleep in most days in the summer. This morning I barely heard Kenny T's truck back out the gravel driveway on his way to work. He must've decided to stop by the diner for breakfast because when I got to the kitchen no coffee was brewing.

Fine, I'd read the newspaper in peace for a change. I boiled some water and made a quick cup of Kava, letting it simmer on the table while I retrieved the morning paper out of the yard. Watchman thumped his bird dog tail on the front porch. I gave him a quick pat, nearly poking his soft nose with the rolled up paper, distracted by the thought of substituting a little peach pie for my biscuit and jelly.

I straightened up, eyeing his full water bowl, but saw that Kenny T had forgotten to put out any dog food in the old stew pot that served as a feeding bowl. How many chances did that man need after all these years? At least Watchman had a forgiving nature.

I flung open the pantry door and dug a big cup into the dog food bag, then stared at all the bare shelves next to it—not a peach pie to be found. Coffee and menopause thrust the heat right on my neck. Shouting at Watchman, "Damn your daddy," I kicked open the front screen and poured kibble into his feed pot.

Watchman's spotted body strained to rise against his spindly legs. I sat down hard on the porch swing and sipped my coffee, listening to his crunch of the kibble. I nudged my foot against the porch boards to hold the swing in place and a little tingle went up my leg. I've felt it more lately, but might have to record it in my spiral diary if it persisted to the annoying stage.

"He's not looking out for either of us today," I said to the dog. Watchman nosed around the stewer and did not even perk his ears.

*

Just as I was finishing a leftover biscuit with jelly, Ruby called—earlier than usual—which was way before Kenny T got home. "I'm leaving town for a couple of days, making a little drive up north to the mountains to check on an old friend."

"Didn't know you knew anybody up that way."

"Long story." Ruby's voice trailed off. Her son was the only person I ever heard tell that she'd make a trip to see.

"Could I go along and hear it?"

"What? You never want to go anywhere for long."

"Right, I'm usually content at home tending to things, but I couldn't calm myself down with another biscuit when I was hankering for a little peach pie. This morning Kenny T took all my peach pies to those gals at the mill. I'm so mad I could spit. His mind is everywhere but at home. I could disappear. It'd teach him a lesson."

"Whoa, are you serious about going?"

"I am. I think I am." I bit my lip and stared at Watchman asleep in Kenny T's recliner. "Yes, I am."

"Then pack your bag. I'll swing by in an hour."

"Just like that?"

"Yep, you said you wanna go."

"Right, okay. I'll get ready. Bye."

"Don't dawdle now. Bye."

I watched the phone fall into its cradle. Letting air fill my stomach and my lungs, I closed my eyes. What if Kenny T would be glad that I was gone? Hmmm, I'd risk it to see his face, when I came waltzing back in a few days. I did a slow dance around the living room, my arms stretching out like limp wings. I jumped, then blew out all my air, thinking someone might be at the door. Watchman had yawned with a little squeal in the back of his throat.

*

I was sitting on my blue Samsonite when Ruby's shiny Ford spun onto the gravel driveway. My salt-and-pepper curls under a pink cowgirl hat were damp from a quick shower. I'd pulled on my favorite orange and pink flowered top and baggy khakis that Kenny T never liked. My red Keds were still untied in the excitement.

Ruby's turquoise ball cap was pulled down over her eyes when she gave a little wave. She had on new jeans and a pressed plaid blouse that I had admired on our last trip to town, but it didn't come in larger sizes.

"Look at that big suitcase. Whoa. We're only gone for a couple days."

"I'm out of practice."

I bumped the big bag down the front steps, trying not to miss Kenny T's help. Shoving a key in the big trunk lid, Ruby giggled as I hurled my suitcase inside. We both slammed the lid down and stared at each other a moment in our traveling clothes.

"What in the hell are we doing?" I laughed, blinking excitedly.

"I'm game," Ruby nodded, pinching her eyebrows close.

*

For the first hour riding on the four lane headed north, my neck was twisting from side to side, watching Ruby's every move. She wasn't the best driver.

"Looky there," she tried to distract me.

My back against that plastic seat was damp, so I leaned toward the little bitty vents seeping air conditioning. I kept rattling my head off about how I came unglued that Kenny T even acted like he might be thinking of any of those gals at the mill and then had the gall to take them my peach pies.

"Uh-huh," she said every few minutes. She sounded like she was listening. Just as well, since usually I have to listen to all of her talk about the County Clerk's office goings-on.

Those late-night calls when she probably had a nip, after all her work gossip, she let me know how bad she missed her husband, who died in a car accident when he was just forty-two, same age as Elvis. It made us closer, especially when I told her I was worried about Kenny T's wandering, though it was no comparison to her woe.

At a stop sign, Ruby stared right at me and said, "Don't you think Kenny T might be upset when he gets home? You didn't even leave him a note."

"I hope so." I blinked, surprised that my throat tightened up. It'd kill me if he wasn't. "Maybe I'll call him at the next stop."

Right after Ruby turned on to the two lane, she made a jerky left swerve up under the rickety canopy hunching over faded gas pumps at a Shell station. My car door flew open, and my hat almost blew back inside the car. I stood up, floating out of my seat. The sweet scent of fresh-cut hay drifted from the field that stretched out full of big mounds way behind the station. Walking around oil smudges toward the edge of the expanse, I imagined driving a big green tractor into the high yellow growth until we both disappeared.

"You been in there?" Ruby was heading toward a battered door with *Ladies* hand lettered in drippy white paint.

I glanced in her direction. "Almost." Then I let myself linger out there in that sweet-scented field, feeling only the tug of the string against my throat from my pink cowgirl hat flapping in the breeze.

"What? You're daydreaming."

I waved toward the door. "Go on. Never mind me."

"I do mind you," Ruby almost whispered. "Did you call Kenny T?"

"No answer." I sniffed.

*

Not long after Ruby steered the Ford back on the road, she pointed to a weathered board sign chiseled with *Jacob's Cave* in fancy blue letters nailed to an aging tree trunk.

"Ever been in a cave?" She turned her head to one side and waited a second, then switched her gaze to the two lane.

"Nope, Kenny T hated closed in places. I never had occasion to consider it. You?"

"Luray Caverns in Virginia, big as a stadium under there, so cold you have to wear a jacket, beautiful rock formations with lights shining on them in a way to make the jagged parts look like a dragon or a fountain." Ruby's head was bobbing with a passion I hadn't often seen in her except when she was riled up about county politics.

"Were you scared being way down under the ground?"

"Naw, they guide you in a big group. Wanna stop at that Jacob's Cave? I've never been."

"It'd be cooler than in here. Why not?"

I sat up a little taller in the seat, yet was queasy in the knees about this decision, then strained to watch for the next sign. A lone blue arrow painted on a skinny board directed us down a gravel drive.

"Turn here."

The Ford lunged at a muddy pothole, and Ruby let the steering wheel spin in her hand.

"There's a little shop, but no signs."

Ruby made a sharp turn into an open lot in front of a small log building and pulled up alongside a lone pickup truck. A *Closed* sign hanging on the door quickly was turned to *Open*.

"Did you see that sign flip?" I giggled.

Ruby nodded, then laughed out loud. "Whooeee."

We stood on the porch a minute and peered inside a big picture window into a rustic gift shop packed with tourist trinkets. The beaded belts on a stand caught my attention. Maybe I could get matching moccasins. I hadn't bought a souvenir of anything in years, and a smile popped right to my lips when I turned to Ruby.

"We can shop at least if the cave is already closed."

Ruby frowned but pushed open the door. Bells attached to the handle jingled like pebbles thrown down a well. With his head cocked to one side, a short fellow about our middling age stood behind a glass display case, motioning us in with a stubby arm. Ruby went right up to him.

"Can we still see the cave?"

He looked like a farmer in worn overalls and a shrunk-up white T-shirt that he'd tried to stretch at the arms. His white hair was thinning, but scraggly white eyebrows couldn't hide crystal blue eyes. He looked out of them like he knew we could not resist looking back.

"Just the two of you?"

His deep voice surprised me coming out of such a short fellow. We nodded and leaned forward over the counter kind of hopeful, still staring right into his cool-as-a-mountain-stream eyes.

"That'd be six dollars apiece for the last tour of the day."

Ruby pulled out some bills quick from her purse. I fumbled through my bag for mine, my fingers jerky with excitement, but my breath caught up with a tad of disap-pointment. "I guess we can shop after the tour."

Ruby tapped my wrist with her keys and said, "We want to get to the cave."

"Better put those keys in your pocket." I had to come back at her.

After we dropped our bills on the counter, Mr. Blue Eyes stood there counting in slow motion. I gazed at the tiny colored stones individually taped to pieces of cardboard inside the display counter. Drumming her fingers on the counter, Ruby could hardly contain her excitement.

"So, where's the cave?"

The fellow grinned for the first time, shoved the money in his pocket, and his stubby arm jerked a large black handle that was attached to the wall behind the counter. Part of the wooden wall slid away on noisy rollers. Cool musty air whooshed out. Our necks stretched forward at the wide expanse of darkness rimmed by chiseled rock behind him.

"Here it is. Come on around behind the counter to go inside. I'm Jake."

Ruby jumped with giddiness and hurried around the end of the counter.

"I'm Ruby. This is Edith."

We nodded. His head dipped down and then side to side like it wasn't totally attached. She started telling Mr. Blue Eyes about all the caves she'd been in and asking how long this one was and what kind of formations we would see.

He swung his arm toward me. "Edith, flip that sign and push the button to lock the front door. I'm here by myself today."

I turned the sign just like a professional employee. Maybe I could quit the school cafeteria and work behind a counter somewhere downtown, but not that old bakeshop Kenny T wanted me to try. I slid my hand along the smooth glass countertop and admired the beaded leather pouches lined up. I followed Ruby's chatty tone inside the cool chamber that was illuminated by a single light bulb hanging a ways from the entrance. We stopped and turned around under the light bulb.

Jake stepped inside and gave the sliding door a hard push, and it rumbled along its rails, closing out the daylight from the shop window. Jake leaned over and picked out some pebbles from the door rail.

"Wouldn't want that door to get stuck."

He turned up a grin of shiny, even teeth, then fumbled with the door, turning several levers, until it clicked.

"Damn, didn't mean to lock it this time a day, but it keeps tourists in the shop from wandering in here while I'm doing a tour. Oh, I've probably got a key."

His clear blue eyes flickered.

"Okaaay," sounded like it stuck in Ruby's throat.

"My cousin usually gives the tour, but we'll make our way through it."

"Sure." I tried to go along with them. Rubbing my palms together, I took a chilly damp breath. "Oh, the cool feels so good."

"I might need a jacket." Ruby moved her hands up and down her arms fast a couple times.

"I won't let you get that cold." Jake made a little noise, maybe a sneeze, and let his short arm drape Ruby's shoulder for a quick minute, then he stepped back away from the light.

Ruby and I gave each other a hurried glance. I wasn't real sure about what this guy knew.

"Follow me, ladies."

Jake started walking ahead of us down a dark tunnel reaching out to flip switches in hidden areas. At a couple stops, he had to run his hand over the tops of several rocks to find the switches. Small light bulbs popped on in crevices along the walls. My toes pressed against my Keds, and the tingling started up in my leg while I tried to take careful steps when the path dipped into a steep descent. Jake's heavy voice droned on about when his cousin bought the cave and how many Indian bones had been found way in the back that he'd let us see if he remembered which tunnel they were in. Just then, his head collided with a jutting rock from the low ceiling, and he cursed.

"Hmm, sorry, ladies. Watch your head. It gets narrow here, might have to crouch just to get through this part."

Ruby touched Jake's back to not lose sight of him as he inched through the passage. Her shoulders bent forward, and I leaned toward her back to see the dim light in front of her that Jake held. We all did the hokey-pokey moving in the damp little channel, but I was too uneasy to sing. After brushing against wet rocks, I was glad to straighten up at the other end, being taller than both of them. Maybe Kenny T was right about the eeriness of closed-in places.

Ruby stopped to stare at some of the rocks behind the lights, but I never saw any familiar looking animal shapes like she had at Luray. I was just glad to be cool, but unsure what else there was to see and how long we needed to be down there. After about twenty minutes of cave discovery and excavation stories, Jake stopped in a wider expanse and flipped a large switch near a metal box. The cave went dark—pitch black.

"Have you ever been anywhere so dark?" Jake's voice echoed against the rocks. "Sometimes it's romantic being in the dark with someone that you're just getting to know."

I felt for Ruby's hand, and she gripped mine tight though we couldn't even make out our own shadows standing next to each other. I listened to our tiny breaths for nearly a minute before I could muster, "Nope, can't say as I have."

"Could be a power outage. I've got a flashlight to find my way back. What about you two?" Jake's deep laugh was unsettling.

Swatting my neck when a feathery wisp lingered, I reached into the darkness. Did he circle around behind us, caught up in that romantic talk? I shuddered. Then it hit me. We were way off a back road, underground. Not a soul knew where we were. We were fools. A vision of Kenny T's ashen face hanging over my casket popped in my head. Overwhelmed that I might never touch his cheek again, my knees began to give way, and I leaned into Ruby.

"That's not funny, Jake. I know the guide always turns out the lights on a tour, but now you need to flip that breaker right back on." Ruby's voice started squeaky but came on strong. "Right, Edith?"

"Uh-huh," I managed in support.

Jake shined his flashlight around the craggy ceiling and then to the metal box and pulled the switch. "I was just funning you." His light eyes were almost back in view.

"We're ready to turn around," I whined without even asking Ruby.

"We can skip the Indian bones," Ruby affirmed.

Jake made a little chuckle. "Hmm, let's see if I know the way back."

Swinging the beam from his flashlight over our faces, he brushed past us, the lingering sent of strong tobacco on his overalls. He managed strides longer than it had seemed his short legs could carry him earlier and barely talked. Twice he turned down rocky little paths with water dripping from overhead, but he couldn't find a light switch or maybe he was lost.

"This isn't how a tour goes," Ruby whispered to me.

"He's really creepy," I said real low next to her ear.

We tried for small talk, but our voices were shaky. How tall is the ceiling? What minerals are still present? Are there bats? Jake made a few grunts. We all panted at the vigorous pace and the uphill climb through the damp chambers, but I didn't think twice about resting since I didn't want to lose sight of our crazy guide.

Then I caught sight of that lone light bulb in front of the door. We shifted on our feet trying for calm and not yelling out that he nearly scared us to death. Jake jiggled the lock, cursing, eventually asking me to hold his flashlight on it. He held up a string of keys and started trying each one in the lock. About halfway through the string, a little key snapped the lock. We pushed wildly against the door. Nothing happened. Ruby screamed in panic. I was getting ready to.

"Hold on." Jake's voice went deeper in agitation.

He flipped two small levers and heaved the door so hard on its rails that the clatter was piercing. We scurried past Jake into the light of the shop like frantic insects exposed under a rock. I was the first to the outside door, twisting the handle desperately to pop the lock in the knob. Ruby was pushing against my shoulders with her frigid fingers.

"Didn't you want to buy a souvenir?" Jake called to us.

We didn't look his way. After Ruby slammed the door hard enough to rattle its glass, I glanced back at the beaded belts through the window. Ruby tugged at my arm while she ran down the steps toward the car. The *Closed* sign still was swinging like a pendulum while Ruby gunned the motor and tore out of the parking lot.

"We were absolute fools to go in there alone, Ruby."

My hands were shaking in my lap.

"I'm so sorry to take you in there. It wasn't supposed to be like that."

Ruby's eyes welled up, and she couldn't stop her watery nose. I dug for my whole pack of tissues in my purse.

"I just can't believe we did that."

My body was fighting hot and cold flashes at once. I burst out into a flood that dampened my flowered blouse. We rode a few miles alternating between wails and laughter. We were both snorting into the last of a pile of tissues when Ruby pulled into the Texaco.

"I'm about to pee my panties."

She disappeared behind the building in pursuit of a ladies' room. I spied a pay phone and called Kenny T.

"Baby, I nearly lost my life. I'm so grateful for you even if you did take all my pies to those mill gals."

"Where are you, Edith? It's nearly dark." His throat sounded tight, almost choky. "It's not like you to be gone. I was starting to worry." Then he coughed. "Your pies are at Angela's Bakeshop. Over two dozen sold. See, I told you."

"Really?" My heart went to pounding, proud that he was concerned and that folks liked my pies. I glanced over at Ruby in the car and wondered if she'd had enough for one day. Ruby gave a thumbs-up.

"What happened to the rest of the pies?" I chewed my lip, calmed by my husband's familiar nature but uneasy about what else he'd been up to.

Kenny T made a whiney reply. "I ate some more and shared a few."

"Hmm, sharing with those gals? What has gotten into you acting like that again?"

"What about you? You're the one gone. Probably Ruby put you up to this behavior."

"Nope, it was totally my idea. Just like you deciding to take all my pies."

"I was trying to help."

"I believe you, honey, but..." A sour taste came to my mouth, knowing he didn't do it just for me, and that's what hurt. "I'm glad folks bought the pies, but I think you're being kinda selfish more than helping. So I'll use the pie money to pay my way on this trip with Ruby."

"Edith, I'll make it up to you."

"I know you'll try, baby. See you Thursday, Kenny T."

The Sewing Machine

The two women drove up to the Shell gas station in their black Ford and waved at us.

"They must be the ones," I said, tugging at my bra and the tight shorts sticking to my legs. I crawled out of my truck uneasily.

"Glad they showed up," my girlfriend Gina said.

I made a quick yank on the old motorcycle straps I had wound around the wooden sewing machine case that fastened it to the truck bed. Was I ready?

The woman in the Ford's passenger seat rolled down the window and stuck out a head of bouncy curls. "Let's see it."

She pushed herself out of the car and leaned against it, stomping her right foot against the concrete. "Darn neuropathy, that's what they call what I got. That tingling slows me down."

The driver dressed in a plaid top and baggy jeans rushed toward my truck, a straw handbag in one hand and a can of Coke in the other, announcing, "I'm Ruby."

She jerked her head toward her friend. "Edith's the one who's been writing to you on the computer."

Edith massaged her leg and made a little wave.

I nodded and said, "I'm Lorraine." The words came oozing out of my mouth like a third grader. Why didn't I say Raine, a name I've claimed since college? I wiped a sweaty palm on my shorts and pointed. "That's Gina."

Gina wiggled one finger toward us and made a goofy smile.

Edith waddled toward the truck, pushing a white patent handbag up on her thick sleeveless shoulder.

"Let's see if it looks like your pictures on Craigslist."

"Okay."

Since she was a little bossy, I hesitated a minute, then took a breath. My fingers fumbled to loosen the straps. Finally I pulled away the old quilt, letting it drape into a mound around the wooden legs. The polished wooden case glistened in the sun. I squinted up at it, my eyes watery and stinging.

"Ah..." they both exclaimed.

Edith clapped her hands and leaned in closer. "Let's see the machine inside."

I climbed into the truck bed, the leaf springs giving into my weight and jostling the truck bed, but the heavy case barely shifted, though it caused me to almost lose my balance. I careened forward, hugging the top of the wooden case. It scooted, but didn't topple, almost like it didn't want to go.

Gina held up her arms. "Hold it, hold on."

Hovering over the case, I yelled, "Got it."

Gina kicked aside the quilt, pushed the dangling electric cord back up inside, and helped me lower the machine to the ground. I raised the wooden lid and swung up the heavy black machine head. The women crowded in.

"Whoa," said Edith. "Now that's about the prettiest..."

Ruby poked Edith's shoulder with the Coke can and whispered, "Not so fast."

The sun's rays made me swimmy-headed. I sank down on the tailgate after Ruby's hesitation. How long would these women argue? I thought it was time to let this machine go. I began to think about how hard that decision was to make.

*

Yesterday Gina and I had decided to take spring cleaning seriously. I had been upstairs all morning sorting through kitchen cupboards. The buzz of saws and laughter drifted up the basement stairs occasionally interrupting the top tunes blaring from the old radio. Gina and Margie were building new shelves for a workshop down there which meant dragging long stored treasures and a good bit of trash to the center of the garage part of the basement.

Finally they called, "Raine, bring the camera."

My next job was posting pictures to Craigslist to sell whatever had been uncovered. When I came down the steps, Gina was wide-eyed.

"Do you want to sell that?"

*

Mama's sewing machine was probably the last thing Gina and I had loaded into the U-Haul truck over twenty years ago when we sold my parents' home in Mississippi and moved them to Texas so I could look after them. That day Mama was finishing up a pinstriped vest for Daddy while we moved boxes all around her. "Don't rush me. It'll be done before we need to leave," she kept saying, but she spent the afternoon ripping out seams and re-sewing them until she was exhausted, finally leaning her head next to the machine and sobbing. Helpless, I touched her back and waited, breathing quick to keep myself together. After sunset, we dragged the heavy machine case up the rental truck ramp, heaved it against the mattresses, and pulled down the door, closing out the light to the family possessions.

Yesterday the dusty wooden case with four spindly wooden legs sat exposed, out of place, on our oil-stained garage floor. I glanced at it and didn't want to remember the day I brought it from the senior living apartment into this garage. That meant Mama was dead and the machine was something I didn't know what to do with. I hadn't touched that case—not even opened it—since then. I told myself I didn't sew, but then worried. It was my last tangible reminder of Mama.

I said to Gina, "Crazy to leave it down here any longer. It's time."

Gina turned down the radio and walked over closer.

I snapped a picture of the case, then exhaled. "I won't need your help here."

My stomach nervous, I ran my hand across the dusty top, then along the cobweb-entangled legs. Shame crept hot up my back as I assessed my neglect of Mama's prized possession.

"It's in good shape," Gina offered.

"Not by Mama's standards," I retorted, my tone defensive.

"I could..." Gina tried.

I waved Gina back to her work. I managed a barely audible, "I'll get some pictures, see what we've got here."

I stepped closer and wiped my dusty hands on a rag from a nearby box. Pulling up the wooden top, I laid it open and snapped a picture. The dark machine inside the case lay as quiet as Mama in her grave. They both had stopped together, and I felt the loss again like on moving day. Her memory had not left, remaining on the machine somewhere between the needle and the little black wheel she turned so often.

I turned to Gina. "Sorry, I hadn't expected this."

"It's okay." Gina's smile was bleak.

Reaching inside the case, I gripped the shiny black neck of the machine and swung the heavy weight up out of its dark stowage, pushing down the small wooden holder in front for it to balance on. It was a motion I had seen Mama make effortlessly so often that I was surprised at the machine's heaviness. Oil residue moistened my fingers. I snapped a picture, but the angle was wrong. I zoomed in on the ornate gold lettering of Singer and the swirling golden-painted decorations stretching across the ebony body, rich yet ancient in design. Its beauty rivaled the beautiful clothing Mama had created through the years. Snap, snap of the camera captured the machine but not the shadows I glimpsed around it.

I emptied furniture polish found in the rag box onto an old cloth and watched my hands shaped like Mama's bring the wood back to the life that she often gave it. The dark stain left an oily familiar smell, making a tinny taste in the back of my throat. I imagined Mama pulling a pair of summer shorts out from under the pressure foot of the machine, then me modeling them, turning in little circles. I loved the shorts, but didn't want to learn to make them.

*

Today I swung my legs nervously from the tailgate. Fluttering in the wind, a piece of blue thread remained in the needle. I didn't recognize the color.

"That polish is scraped off," Ruby said. "There's a little dent in the top."

I shifted on the tailgate, then stood up, noticing the finish worn away from the wooden case in front of the open machine where Mama had pulled many a fabric through.

I sighed, "Mama leaned the lid against the machine, liked to leave it open more than closed."

Ruby's head shot up. "This was your Mama's? Why, girl, how can you bear to part with it?" She wiped her brow with a kerchief from her straw bag and took a long drink of Coke.

I slipped on sunglasses from my pocket. "I don't sew—had it a long time since she's passed away."

Edith stroked the shiny black machine. "Aww, I'll take good care of it for you, don't you worry. Gee, I wished my Mama had sewed. We're going to start a quilting bee and..."

"Well, I guess you've bought it." Ruby frowned and leaned back on her Ford's fender. "Would you take less?"

I chewed my lip. "I did bring it this far for you. I think it's a fair price."

Edith snapped open her white bag and pulled out a hundred-dollar bill. "Here you go. I want it."

Ruby swung her arm in front of Edith, the Coke can bending in her hand. "I can't guarantee that I'm joining this quilting bee, just so you know."

Edith folded the bill in half and pursed her lips. "Well, this is a fine time to get cold feet standing out here in the boiling sun. What has come over you, Ruby?"

Her friend drained her Coke and tossed the can inside her car window. Pouting, Ruby fiddled with the knob on the little drawer on the front of the machine.

I raked my fingers through my hair, my eyes blazing toward Gina. "Now, we've driven all this way and..."

Gina rushed over to the machine. While patting my shoulder, she turned to Ruby and Edith. "Need a little time? We're going to walk over to the Quik Mart and get a cold drink. Y'all try to decide on this purchase before we get back, okay?"

Edith hung her head, whining, "I can't believe this is happening."

I slapped my thigh and glared back at the old women while Gina hurried our steps toward the mart. Glancing again over my shoulder, I caught Ruby peering into the machine drawer.

Mama had long since taken out her little scissors and the yellow measuring tape. There was nothing to steal, I assured myself, and they couldn't lift it by themselves. I pushed open the door to the mart. Cool air swirled around my head.

*

Clutching icy bottles of water, we came around the black Ford and found the two women sitting on my truck tailgate. Edith struggled to reach the ground.

"Can't sit still and think too long. Neuropathy nearly froze up this leg," she said. "I'm ready to go."

She pushed the folded bill into my hand. Her spiky eyebrows wiggled while her gray eyes squinted directly into mine. "Honey, I'm sorry we acted a fool. I'm proud to own your mama's machine."

Ruby kept her head down, opened up the Ford trunk, and spread out a tattered blanket for the machine to lie on. The sun glinted against the gold insignia, the machine nearly burning my hand when I folded it down into the case. Our shirts wet from the strain, Gina and I eased the heavy machine into the trunk, pulled the blanket over the top, and gave it a final pat. With twine Edith handed me, I tied down the trunk lid over the protruding legs. We all stood behind the Ford, staring into the little open space of trunk.

"What was your mama's name?" Edith shifted her weight to her good leg.

I winced, but managed, "Lucille—she'd liked Cele."

"We name all the machines at the quilting bee. I'll name this one Cele."

I imagined Mama sticking out her heavenly tongue at this suggestion. My throat stayed tight. I just patted Edith's bare shoulder.

"Guess that'll do it," Edith said, holding out her hand.

I shook her hand and nodded. "It will."

I gave the folded bill an extra squeeze inside my pocket. Thinking about Mama hiding special things in strange places, I turned toward the women and asked, "You didn't find anything in that little machine drawer, did you?"

Ruby's head shot up, then she shook it. "Nope."

I leaned over and made a last peek inside the trunk.

"Better be going," Ruby said, slamming the driver's door.

Slowly moving back toward my truck, Gina and I watched the two women pull onto the highway, the machine legs sticking out from the Ford's trunk. Ruby honked the horn. I gave a little wave good-bye.

Endless Errors

*E*dith was trying to talk to her health insurance company, but the first nice lady on the line didn't understand her urgency. She told her to wait, and Edith had been on the phone for close to ten minutes listening to some loud piano playing, with an occasional break with a recorded voice saying all representatives are busy, please keep holding. Edith tried not to stare at the clock's second hand over the sink. Brushing a moist cheek with her free hand, she broke down when a live human spoke into her ear, all perky like she was having the best time answering folks' calls.

"This is Tiffany. How can I help you?"

"Oh, lord, thank you..." And Edith grabbed for a tissue to catch her wet nose and spoke in a crinkly voice, "I've been waiting so long, honey. My hand is sweaty from holding up this receiver to my ear. I'm scared I'm going to lose my insurance, and I can tell that some nausea is about to come on. I've got a serious condition. The doctor said..."

"Just tell me your name? I'm going to have to get your information." Tiffany got right to the point.

"Didn't the first lady tell you who I was?"

"No, that's a different department."

Edith groaned but rattled off her life history and part of her mama's history. A girl with the name of Tiffany shouldn't be old enough to hear all that. Why didn't they already know her?

"It's security, ma'am, just trying to verify you are a legitimate policy holder." Tiffany sounded a little huffy. Then she put Edith on edge when she came back on the line saying, "Your premium is past due this month."

Edith wheezed, "I got a letter about that, but no, that's not true. I have my bank statement right here that shows you took out too much money—well, not you personally. I never liked that automatic withdrawal idea, and I don't..."

Tiffany snapped, "Hold on, I'll have to transfer you to billing."

The music started again in Edith's ear. Sighing, she switched the receiver to her left hand. "I hope the next one is friendlier," she told Watchman. The bird dog her husband might love more than Edith halted in the doorway and sniffed. "Daddy filled your bowl," Edith responded, staring at the damp muzzle. That dog must have gone to the water trough on the porch first.

She scooted her chair nearer the wall and rested her head against the cool plaster. Her eyelids hung heavy from little sleep since she discovered the billing error, and then there were the bouts of nausea. The sporadic tap of Watchman's toenails on the linoleum made a little rhythm with the music in her ear.

The tapping was like Kenny T's fishing reel inching over each sprocket. He let her try it out on their first date over ten years ago. She stood on the dock and threw the line as far as she could, letting the red and white bobbin that held up the almost invisible fishing line float only a few seconds. Then she turned the little crank and reeled the line back in. She didn't want to wait for the fish to bite. Laughing, Kenny T just dropped in a cane pole so they'd have something for supper. She liked that about him, just letting her have fun.

"Billing, this is Sierra." The nasally tone stirred Edith.

"Sahara, like the desert?"

"Uh, huh, no, like the mountains," came after a windy breath from Sierra.

"Hmm, interesting...anyway, can you look up how much money came to you from my account at Farmer's Bank? It was January 8, Elvis's birthday. How about that!"

Sierra was all business. "Verify your mother's maiden name for me."

Edith repeated the maiden name, a disturbing reminder that her mama had not returned her calls during the winter holidays. Her mama had nearly died in the operating room over a year ago, though she had assured Edith beforehand that her gall bladder surgery was no cause for Edith to worry. So she didn't pace in the waiting room while her mama lay on a cold operating table. Instead she went fishing with Kenny T and called the hospital when she got home. A distance had grown between them after that with fewer calls. Her mama, in a chilly tone, had declared Kenny T inconsiderate as well. Now Edith didn't feel like she could tell her mama her fears about her own health issues. She wondered how to make it up to her.

Clicking started. Sierra must be at a keyboard with a computer in front of it like Edith saw in her friend Ruby's office in the courthouse. Banks had computers too. People had them in their homes. Edith was not sure why, and her husband Kenny T didn't care about learning how to work it, so they weren't getting one. His glasses steamed up when he had to stand in a line at Sears waiting for the sales clerk to learn how to log his payment in the new computer. After that he told Edith to talk to them when computers were involved. That was fine with her. She could talk to anyone.

"Sahara...Sierra, hello?" No response except that incessant clicking.

When Ruby called her in the evenings, she was always "wore out" using her computer. Ruby said, "There's so much to remember how to operate it, and it never quits giving me work." The mystery of computers is a sign of the 1980s they agreed and went on to talk about the people they knew. Watchman often thumped his tail expectantly if she neared his food bowl while she paced the kitchen talking to Ruby, then eventually the dog retreated to Kenny T's recliner in the living room if he wasn't in it.

Edith reminded Ruby that her own job could be wearing, standing on her feet all day. Since she was just in her forties, the older women left heavier tasks to her, pulling endless trays of cornbread out of the school cafeteria oven and mashing up mounds of creamed potatoes. Wearing a hairnet snapped around her bouncy curls, she hated that "old lady" shape the net made. In white uniforms with sweating foreheads, she and the other women stood behind the steam tables serving four shifts of students shuffling by in a chattering mass, hardly glancing at their meal providers. The neighbor girl and her impish little friend always smiled. Ruby didn't like that girl's mama, but Edith reminded her that the girl must have learned something from her mama. She was always polite in the cafeteria and said, "Hi, Miss

Edith." Edith laughed to herself about the girl's crooked smile. The desire to bear children had not waned, but adoption scared her.

What a difference a sweet glance or a greeting made. Maybe this Sierra was that kind of young lady. Edith exhaled and turned toward a scraping noise. Watchman nosed his almost-empty bowl up next to the wall to capture the final morsels.

The clicking in her ear stopped. Edith picked up her bank paper again to read along. Sierra was frustrated. "Your payment had been credited to another person's account. We have a new computer system. That's probably the reason."

Edith's breathing sped up. Money problems always raised her blood pressure, though she hid her frustrations from Kenny T. Keeping his trust was most important to her, and she hoped he'd be trustworthy himself. He carried a lot of cash that she couldn't keep track of. He wanted the guys to bet on the outcome of every pick-up basketball game they played a few nights every week.

Sierra's voice turned sunny, but abrupt. "I moved the correct amount into your account, so now you're up to date. I'm closing this ticket."

Relief calmed Edith for a brief moment, but then she remembered the double payment. "Wait, what about that extra money that was taken? I need that back."

Sierra was frustrated again. "Just a moment."

Edith heard muffled voices on the line. Her neck tightened, and she tried to wiggle it around with her shoulders pushing up toward her ears. A jumpy little nerve in her leg tingled like that fishing line snapping back into the reel over the shimmery water. Lost money made a dark hole in her confidence.

When they were driving to town right after they were married, Kenny T gave her his paycheck from the mill. Later that day at the bank, she was frantic when the check was not in her purse. She even dumped it upside down at the teller's booth, embarrassing herself and everyone else in the bank with all her junk and more when a Kotex sanitary pad rolled out and dropped by her feet. She never found that check, and by the time she told Kenny T, he had written a couple bad checks on the household account, thinking the money was there. She gasped and hoped he hadn't done that recently.

Edith's stomach tumbled with the memory. Kenny held on to the money-managing quite a while after that before dealing with the computers started getting to him. Edith felt so foolish. That's when she went to the drugstore and bought a spiral notebook and began to write down all of her feelings about the mystery of that lost check and other things that confused her. She hoped there would not be plenty to write about this mix up, but she knew she'd fill a page when her current medical ordeal was over. She chewed her lip and waited for the voices to stop on her phone and one to talk to her.

"Hey, this is Mabel."

"Oh, no, am I going to have to explain this whole problem all over again?"

Edith sat back down and worried all this tension might just bring on her period early this month. It wasn't even her fault, and she'd have to tell Kenny T about the billing mess.

A helpless voice squeaked from her, "Please get my money back."

Mabel said, "What was that date that had something to do with Elvis?"

"His birthday. I noticed the withdrawal came on January 8."

"Hmm, my grandmother drove all the way to Graceland when he died. Did you?"

Edith nodded like Mabel was in the room and relaxed her tight fingers on the receiver. "I thought about it, but my husband would have thought I was crazy." Edith laughed and Mabel joined in.

"Yeah, just as well. My granny said it was a blubbering madhouse out by his gate—hot too. Be right back." The clicking started again.

Edith liked the sound of Mabel's voice. She stretched the phone cord so she could reach inside the fridge for a Coke. She took a long fizzy drink that made her belch and covered the receiver, not to be rude. The clicking stopped.

"Now, honey, we've got this sorted out. I'm reversing the additional funds from the wrong account and posting them as credit to your account. Next month's premium will be already paid."

Edith cringed, as bewildered as a caged dog. "I don't want to pay a month ahead."

Edith worried that if she didn't survive the surgery she was scheduled to have next week, there wouldn't be enough money in the bank to bury her. She slammed the Coke on the table.

"The computer won't let me send the money back to your bank account."

"My bank account might be overdrawn," Edith whined. She dreaded calling the bank to really find out.

"Hold on, I'll try something," Mabel said, this time turning the music on in Edith's ear.

Edith took another swig of Coke. This Mabel loved her granny and probably had a good family. She looked out for the ones she talked to. She could feel it. Edith listened to the same music and tried to imagine what Mabel looked like.

She sighed when the music stopped. "There had been a Mabel in my high school class. She died when her car ran right into the Tennessee River at one of those boat ramps."

"Uh, huh, common name. Lordy, that's a tale. Hold on." Mabel was abrupt.

The violins in the phone music squealed like poor young Mabel must have, before the water rushed into her car. Edith pulled the receiver away from her ear. Her head spun a moment before she sat down.

For her next surgery, Edith feared the plastic cup the nurse would put over her nose and mouth, almost choking her for a minute, before the anesthesia helped her no longer worry and push out a little trust that the doctor knew what he was doing. When she was forty, her appendix sent rippling pains down her side. It was her first surgery. Since it took a year to pay off the bill, she made Kenny T sign up for insurance for both of them at the mill.

Now the doctor said her gall bladder had to come out within the next week. Kenny T was lucky nothing was ever wrong with him. He sat in the waiting room reading Field and Stream with an ear open for some town news while she thumbed through Reader's Digest. She looked for the jokes to distract her attention from the ache in her side, always wary of a sharper pain that might stay longer.

After her examination, she calmed herself and whispered the new surgery news to Kenny T. His eyes blinked, then he pressed lips on her neck for a long moment.

He whispered, "It'll be okay." Then he patted her leg and said, "We've got insurance, right?"

Edith nodded but decided to check the bank withdrawal when she got home, just in case. Then the past due notice came, which added to the confusion. That's what started all this.

Watchman ambled toward her, rested his head in her lap a minute, then licked her hand. Edith patted his bony head and wiped the wet on her apron. The music stopped.

Mabel's voice was smiling. "I'm sending you a refund check, but we'll have to create a new policy number."

"Oh, it can't come to my house. Can I pick it up at my agent's office this week?"

Mabel coughed. "I'm doing the best I can. The computer can't release funds until the first of next month after the new policy number is created and the other policy is cancelled."

Edith tugged hard on her bouncy curls, then let go and slumped back in her chair. She couldn't risk cancelling anything.

"Never mind. Just go ahead and credit it to next month's premium so my husband won't get a bill. In case I'm dead by then, he'll just have to use his own money to bury me."

"Okay, that'll probably work out better for you. Is there anything else now?" Mabel didn't sound expectant.

"No, not that you can do anything about." Edith almost chuckled and leaned back in her chair. When the dial tone buzzed in her ear, she sat up, blinking in surprise. She thought Mabel was friendlier than that.

Edith dropped the phone in the cradle and groaned. Watchman's head popped up from his outstretched paws. Edith bent over and ruffled the warm fur on his back, saying, "I'm going to have to go through with the surgery now. You take care of Daddy if I don't make it." Watchman's tail thumped, and he made a little moan as he stretched out into his full length.

*

Later in the week, when Edith came down the stairs from the bedroom, Kenny T was munching a cold biscuit that he'd probably dipped in the jelly jar. "Thanks for such a big batch of biscuits. Sorry you can't eat before surgery, honey." He leaned at an awkward angle on the front door licking the biscuit edges to keep the jelly from slipping. He eyed Watchman asleep in his recliner and then Edith.

"I've made casseroles and a big batch of my special brownies. You won't have anyone to cook for you." Edith's throat tightened, thinking of Kenny T eating by himself.

She dropped her eyes away from him and pulled her Sunday coat from the hall closet. A sharp pain gouged into her right side. Edith gasped, and her face contorted. She swung open the front door and gulped the icy February air. "I guess this is how it goes."

Kenny T's eyes widened and he shoved the rest of the biscuit in his mouth, mumbling, "Let's get in the truck and head to the hospital. I'm glad there'll be something to eat in the house when I get home. Thanks, honey."

*

Inside the hospital admittance office, Edith and Kenny T sat together across the desk from a stout woman in a bright green blouse. Tiffany Washington was etched on a small nameplate pinned to her matching sweater. Edith stared at the name and squirmed, taking shallow breaths to manage the pain in her side. She pushed her insurance card and her driver's license across the desk. Kenny T twisted his Rubik's cube.

Tiffany's thin lips parted into a brief perfunctory smile. Her short fingers moved over a keyboard, and the bright screen she stared at reflected on her shiny cheeks. When the clicking stopped, she announced, "Your insurance policy is in arrears. Would you like to speak with someone in our credit department?"

"What?" Kenny T dropped his cube, his neck twisting toward Edith.

Edith squealed and leapt from her seat. "No, that's all been corrected last week. I talked to Tiffany, then Sahara. No, it was Mabel that settled it."

"No ma'am, you didn't talk to me. Have a seat. Now let me make a phone call."

"Ask for Mabel." Edith leaned over the desk grasping her painful side.

*

Kenny T waved bye with the Rubik's cube when Edith moved inside the small pre-op changing room. Before she could protest, Edith's head swirled while she laid on the gurney, blinking at bright ceiling lights.

"Tell Mable she needs to go with me to see Elvis. He'll pay for everything."

Two women with funny green hats leaned over her.

"Is Mabel in the waiting room with Kenny T? It would serve her right to have to sit there." Edith giggled. "Kenny T better not run off with her." Edith frowned, then laughed. "He won't be able to find her on the phone."

*

An irritating "click click" of some equipment whined nearby, interrupting Edith's attempt to stay asleep. Her head was heavy as a boulder when she moved it to the side. She peeked through one eye at a steel rail alongside where she was lying.

"She's awake. Tell me your name," a distant voice prodded.

"Edith T..."

"Good. Maybe some tea later, Edith. We'll take you out of recovery now. Your surgery is over." A figure in white stretched over her. Edith squeezed her eyes shut when she felt movement, then nausea.

The next time Edith peered through her eyes, two figures were whispering in the corner of her room. "Mama, is that you with Kenny T?"

Edith's mama pulled photos from Kenny T's hands and waved them over her head. "Looky at your gall stones."

"Don't show her those. It'll make her sick." Kenny T flung his arm, making a futile grab for the photos.

Edith's mama waddled toward her bed, blocking Kenny T from her view, and dropped the photos on her daughter's sheet. She leaned in close, her peppermint Chiclets not masking her smoky breath when she said, "See, that surgery is not as easy as you thought. Bet you thought I'd just be fishing, but I knew to be here."

Like a small child, Edith squinted and raised a finger to caress her mama's face. "You don't fish, Mama," she giggled.

She pulled a photo close to her face, then let it float to the floor. "Ooooh, so many marbles. Will I get them back?"

"You don't want those back, honey." Kenny T nudged next to Edith's mama at the bed railing.

Her mama flung her graying curls back and gripped the rail tighter. Her nose tilted up a little when she announced, "Remember, you and Kenny went fishing when I was in the hospital, but I've forgiven you."

Kenny T struggled past Edith's mama, kissed his wife's forehead, and whispered, "Ruby called your mama. I didn't. I mean we didn't want to worry her, but..."

Edith's mama glared at Kenny T. "I was surprised not to at least get a call from you, Kenny T, about my daughter's health. Gall bladder surgery is no joke. I should know. I hope you both learned your lesson about ignoring me."

Kenny T gave Edith an uneasy look.

"You didn't return my calls, Mama. I thought you were ignoring me. I told him not to call you."

"Well, I was ignoring you, so you can forgive me, too."

"Oh, of course I do. I was worried I'd die and never see you again."

Kenny T's face slackened at the suggestion of her death. "We do have life insurance paid up, right?"

Big Chance

riday morning I struggled to lift the plastic shopping bags out of the buggy. I could tell my arms were feeling loose since I retired. I glanced at my reflection in the glass door, then hurried out of the Piggly Wiggly carrying all the last-minute baking ingredients on my wife's list. I wish she hadn't decided to bake three more batches of brownies for the Spring Festival. I hoped for a chance to drop by the mill where I used to work to visit, but thought better of it. I made time to head across the street to city hall after dropping the bags in the truck bed and taking a quick glance in the side mirror to straighten my cap.

Mary Claire waved to me from behind her desk. "Hey, Kenny T." Then she looked over her shoulder and motioned for me to bend over her desk so she could whisper, "I heard the prison work detail might be doing Spring Festival maintenance, just so you know." Her eyes flashed, then fell into a worried gaze.

"Okay," I gulped. "We've got number one, right?"

"Yes, anything for you, Kenny T."

"Okay." I smiled. "See you tomorrow at the booth, right?" I gave her a little wink.

After I got into the truck, I watched the state prisoners— a group of men dressed in white—placing trash cans around the Spring Festival grounds at Bumpas Park, but didn't recognize any of them. I drove home with a prickly twitch in my shoulder.

When I slipped inside the back door, Edith wiped the sweat from her neck with a flowery hankie. She was a trooper. She was frying little pies, apple and peach, for the Spring Festival. Spicy warmth seeped from the oven full of banana bread loaves. I hung around when she started whistling and offering samples. The counter tops, kitchen table, even the TV trays held clumps of brownie dough ready to put in when the loaves came out. Her arms hung heavily, her fingers not as quick molding the dough into shape as when we got married. She was five years older than me and beginning to show it. She was a looker back in the day.

She was smaller now than when she worked in the school cafeteria. She retired in her sixties, but it wasn't her idea, not mine either. The neuropathy in her legs just crept in and weakened her foundation. Since then, I knew I had to stick around for support.

She clicked her teeth when she said, "Kenny T, making sweets is getting to be too much for me, but I know folks will be expecting me at booth number one. I did get booth number one, didn't I?"

"For sure, honey, best corner at the festival," I said to reassure her. "You can spend the day catching up on the courthouse gossip and counting your money."

Besides Spring Festival, she was always trying to find ways to supplement her government check. She wanted to take a drive down to Tate's Store a couple times a week to buy a lottery ticket. She always claimed I never brought home any real money or real news. I did spend a lot on good times.

She wouldn't understand my latest plan, but I found a lot of folks willing to pay for what my brother Leonard can send me. I know it's not legal, but it's a chance I have to take. I won't have to worry about his share since his jail term won't be up for a long time. I can always say I gave it to his girlfriend, Mary Claire, but I'd be scared if it came to that. When I asked him any questions, he threatened to turn me in. But then he joked, "What did working hard all your life ever get you or Edith?" I got that twitch in my shoulder when he talked like that. I didn't have an answer he would take anyway.

Edith worried that her friend Ruby and I got ourselves into too many things that she couldn't keep up with. Ruby called Edith every morning since she got that cell phone. Ruby was always gossiping about where she'd been since she retired from the County Clerk's office. She went to yoga class at the Methodist Church, and I saw her wandering around Orange Hollow center at least once a week. Sometimes Edith called her at night and would say that Ruby's voice sounded different. Could Ruby have taken to drink? After she hung up, Edith wrote little notes to herself in a spiral notebook. She always kept track of things she didn't understand. I was tempted to read it.

Since I retired from the mill a while back, I got in my truck a few times a week to have lunch with the women still working on the line. It was the only time I showered early, used strong smelling aftershave, and put on good hair oil. Edith just didn't pay attention anymore. That neuropathy just took over her mind.

I'm sure it was Ruby who let Edith know a new woman on the line at the mill named Sue was making eyes at me. It must have been when I heard Edith tell Ruby, "I have to trust he'll do the right thing." I was glad to hear her say that.

She knows I love to chatter and flirt. Back when I was still at the mill, Edith asked me why I carried on so, but I just gave a big grin. "I love women. My mama was a woman, you know." We had plenty of arguments, but after the weakness took her legs, Edith finally decided to let it lay.

I knew she thought she had worse things to worry about now. Packages began to appear on the front porch. They were wrapped in the white slicky paper that my brother Leonard got from the meat counters at the jail cafeteria. I kept an eye out, and when a package arrived, I scooped it up, trying to walk quick to avoid being seen. I locked them in a big plywood cabinet inside the tin shed out back. I called that place my shop. It was the place I could keep things to myself.

Edith didn't know where I kept the key. I knew she would not risk walking that far out into the yard to satisfy her curiosity anyway. I found a pair of binoculars in a kitchen drawer. She probably spied on me when I left the shop door open, but there's nothing to see. I'm sure she thinks it's just junk Leonard sends, since she doesn't like him.

I stayed in the kitchen trying to help out more, just to cheer her up, keep her mind off my business. The night before the Spring Festival, I said, "Better get those labels done tonight before you get too tired."

Edith yawned while she sat at the kitchen table and scrawled in shaky script the name of each item and the price, then added "Different but Delicious." She was proud of her unique combinations of chocolate or peanut butter in her banana bread and figs in her brownies. I could eat most of them.

I was ready for bed but peeked from the hallway at Edith ironing her newest old Sunday dress, smoothing out a long slip, and draping her knee-high stockings over her black shoes in our bedroom. She even set the alarm clock on her side of the bed. She slept with her back to me now, deep sleep taking her into noisy bursts of snoring the last few years.

Saturday morning I woke up before the alarm and breathed in the cool morning air slipping under the window. I pulled the bedroom curtain back to check for sunny skies for the Spring Festival. Edith's head was tucked between our pillows, her eyelids wiggling. I pulled on my overalls and slipped into the kitchen, stood at the counter by the window awhile wrapping each pie, loaf, and brownie in cellophane, adding in the little handwritten notes.

I heard the jangle of the alarm. Soon Edith appeared in her chenille robe with her four-pronged cane and steadied herself by the kitchen door. She flipped the switch to the bright light over the metal kitchen table.

"You're up early," she said, her eyebrows spiky, a sleepy glint in her gray eyes.

"I'm about finished," I said, squinting at the bright light. "I've put on all the labels you made. I'll go set up the booth."

Ruby called at her usual time. She kept Edith on the line long enough to prompt several, "I declares." That gave me enough time to get all of the boxes in the truck without her poking around, questioning everything I'd done.

Edith told Ruby, "Come see me at the park. Yes, Kenny T got me booth number one again. I've just been baking night and day." It sounded like she was set in. I pecked her cheek and dashed for the door. "Back to get you soon," I said.

When I was backing out of the driveway, I caught a glimpse of her walking out on the porch. She waved a hankie and threw her spiral notebook toward the driveway. Never saw her do that before. Had Ruby said something to stir her up? If that notebook was there when I got back, I might just have to read it. It'd serve her right for throwing it at me.

I had something to give Sue, so my mind was on a quick trip to town before Edith was ready. I gunned the motor, the truck fishtailing down the road. I drove under a green and yellow Spring Festival banner stretched across the main road into town. Bumpus Park was a tent city, little wisps of morning dew floating in the sunrays over the grassy edges.

I carried a folding table and two chairs from the truck bed to the booth space outlined in bright orange paint on the grass. I pulled an Edith's Kitchen placard from behind the seat and taped the sign to the plastic tent wall of the vendor's booth behind us. I sat one box of food on the table and the others underneath. I counted the boxes, but the one for Sue seemed to be missing, so I decided not to drop by her candle booth.

Had I left her box in the kitchen? I began to worry, rubbing the back of my neck, trying to remember. My hands shook when I placed the home-cooked sweets from one box evenly apart on the tabletop. I sat a big glass jar with Donations Appreciated at the edge of the table. Edith thought she'd get more than her asking price with that jar. Mary Claire would be here soon to help out until we could get back to tend the booth.

A thin finger dug into my shoulder. I turned toward Ruby's powdery pink face smiling from under a straw hat with small bluebirds randomly attached.

"Where's Edith?"

"Wasn't ready." I shot a quick response.

"You helping out today?" Ruby's nose wrinkled. Her cell phone began to sing "Dixie," but she didn't answer.

"Uh, Mary Claire will, she's really helpful." I made a little laugh and blew my nose on a blue bandana. My toes curled inside my boots at the thought of Mary Claire.

Ruby glanced at her phone. "She work at city hall? Think I know her. It's nine fifteen; most folks are set up. I'll look at the other booths. Tell Edith I'll be back to chat before ten o'clock."

"Okay. I'm leaving to get her right quick." I looked past her, my eyes squinting at the morning's rays. Maybe I'd see some women from the line before I left the park.

I moved through the milling crowds, smiling at friendly faces on my way back to the truck. I saw Ruby in the food court, that cell phone pressed against her ear, her hat cocked to shade her eyes.

I drove to the far end of the park. Mary Claire, sitting in her rusty Chevy, gave a quick wave. I stopped and rolled down my passenger window next to her car, pulling a cap over my graying hair to shield my eyes from the sun.

"I'm gonna help out at the booth, just running late checking on festival maintenance." Mary Claire glanced in her rearview mirror, then touched her short curls.

"I've been thinking of you," I said, pushing the gearshift to park but letting the motor idle. My back warmed, and I slid down in my seat to adjust my pants. "Maybe we could take a coffee break later. Got to go back home to get Edith to sit the booth first."

Mary Claire opened her door and moved toward my passenger side window, her flushed cheeks surrounding a pink smile. "Look, I think Leonard might be working at the festival, so maybe not coffee today." Her thick arm rose and bounced her palm off the truck's hood. "Don't forget that."

Over her shoulder, I saw a familiar-looking maintenance man dressed entirely in white, loitering by a nearby garbage can. He kept glancing toward us, then turning around. When I saw State Prisoner was stamped on the back of his T-shirt, I recognized my brother Leonard. He'd seen me with Mary Claire. I belched. A sickly taste crept into my mouth.

When he caught my eye, he ran toward Mary Claire, pushed her inside the cab, and jumped in beside her. His tattooed skinny arm reached across her, jerking the front of my shirt. "I didn't hear if you got the last delivery from that jail trustee. What are you and Mary Claire up to?"

I clutched the wheel, trying to figure out what to say. Mary Claire's nails dug into his leg, and she moaned, "Ohhhh, nooo, Leonard."

"Can you believe I'm out on work detail for good behavior?" Leonard laughed but didn't loosen his grip.

I stared forward, blood pounding behind my eyes, trying to focus on the parking lot, but glanced at Leonard's face. "You're working out in the park?"

"Where have you got my stash, Kenny T?" Leonard let go of my shirt and squeezed Mary Claire's arm. "I thought I could trust you, Mary Claire. You are my girl, the last I remember."

"We didn't do anything wrong, Leonard," Mary Claire squealed.

My mind was spinning. My brother always scared me. "Edith's home. I can show it to you, uh, later."

"You didn't rent a storage locker, idiot?"

Leonard banged his white pants leg against the door. He twisted his neck toward the park, beads of sweat popping out on his neck.

He started mumbling to himself, "I've half a mind to go out there and check the stash. My work buddy'll cover for me."

"You sure he'd do that?" I gave Leonard a crazy look.

He just pounded his knee and shouted, "Just get going, brother. You're giving us a ride."

I pressed the gas too hard. After I let the truck bounce over a curb, I saw a thin box slide from under the seat. Leonard reached down and grabbed a handful of wrapped brownies. A small white square was wrapped up in the cellophane under each brownie. I had drawn a little heart around the word Sue on each one.

"Ah, a sweetheart named Sue?" Leonard laughed.

I gulped, my lips held tight while my teeth chewed the inside of my cheeks. My mind jumped between Mary Claire and wondering how Leonard ever got permission for park work detail.

Mary Claire breathed loudly. "Who's Sue?"

"See there, you're both two timers. Now head for the house," Leonard said, his smirk casting a pall inside the cab.

Ruby's black Ford was parked in our driveway when my truck rumbled to a stop. Edith must've called her cell phone. Edith's spiral notebook was sitting on the Ford's hood. My eye went right to the shop door propped open with a brick.

Ruby and Edith were sitting inside on two wooden barrels. I saw that the plywood cabinet door was pried from its hinges, exposing open boxes of state license plates. My hands ached gripping the steering wheel, just staring at those women laughing and popping brownies in their mouths, each using a license as a plate.

"Now we've got to cut them in," I said to Leonard. I pounded the steering wheel, trying to sound assured, but worry about what to say to Edith made my toes curl inside my boots.

Leonard opened another brownie and crunched the heart-shaped note between his teeth.

"See, Leonard, I have all the plates. Now we better get you back to the park to your work detail. We'll wait to sell these 'til you get out." My stomach was beginning to churn.

Edith shouted from the shop, "Mary Claire, you're supposed to be at my booth. How can I sell my bakery?" Edith began to cry. "You left me on the porch, Kenny T."

Ruby came running up to the truck, her bluebird hat flapping. She grabbed Edith's notebook and waved it toward me. "It's all in here, Kenny T, Edith's notes about all those packages. So I told her I'd help her break open your shop and find out what's inside. Lord, don't you know you're taking a big chance?"

Edith stood up and pointed her four-pronged cane at us. Her cane was shaking when she said, "We've been waiting for you to get back. You'll have to include us in this money-making scheme. I'm sorry it's shady dealing."

Edith sniffed, sat down hard, and reached for another bite of her fig brownie. "Help me out of here, Ruby. I've got to get to my booth to make some honest money." Her shoulders drooped when she looked straight toward me and shook her head. "I knew you were a schemer, but I never thought you'd scheme without me."

I sank down in my seat, the prickly twitch returning to my shoulder. I knew I had gone pretty far this time. I just couldn't guarantee it wouldn't happen again, but I wasn't telling Edith.

Skedaddle

I let my ham and grits get cold. My eye caught on the little thing creeping so carefully through the tall grass out back, a haze of light surrounding it with a familiar glow.

My husband Kenny T looked in the direction I was pointing. "I don't see anything."

Was it an apparition making its presence known to me?

He scraped his chair away from the table, knowing how that irritated me. "I'm full as a tick. Think I'll take a drive to town this morning."

Since he hadn't showered or put on his hair oil, I figured he really was just going to chew the fat with the retired fellows down at Bumpas Park. I worried his past scheming and gallivanting might stir in him again, but after the Spring Festival a while ago, he kept closer to home.

"Good," I whispered and craned my neck to glimpse toward the back steps.

"Hump, that's a first that you're glad I'm going to town," he said as his heavy shoes clumped over the wooden hallway and outside onto the front porch. His old truck groaned before firing.

I watched the creature circle Kenny T's old shop. Then it came in closer, rubbing its biscuit head on the back porch railing. It got close enough into the sunlight that I saw the outline of its little skinny ribs under its tabby hair.

*

Last week when it skittered across our driveway in front of the truck, I thought it was a neighbor cat, just out for a stroll. "Look out for that cat!" I shouted.

Kenny T pushed on the accelerator and said, "Just to keep it moving—but I didn't see a thing."

"You'd feel bad if you kilt it," I said, giving his gas-pedal leg a thump.

"Maybe if I'd seen its dead body," Kenny T started to laugh, then pouted.

*

That critter was being brave enough to get this close to the house. I couldn't just sit in my kitchen filling my stomach and looking at its skeleton poking out from under thin hair.

I struggled to my feet, leaning heavy on the table until I could get my cane situated. The last few years the neuropathy in my legs just crept in and weakened my foundation. I could still make my way to find something for it to eat with Kenny T not here to stop me.

After his bird dog Watchman died, Kenny T said, "That's it, we're done with pets. Mourning is the downside of love."

The dog's passing was too hard on both of us, we thought at the time. That old pup and I watched many a midnight movie together when Kenny T wouldn't stay up with us. He'd jump out of Kenny T's recliner and spread out his spotted body, taking up the rest of the couch next to me and licking popcorn out of my hand.

Kenny T said a new animal would get under my feet and trip me up. If he wasn't home, what would happen?

"I could trip myself if I wasn't watching, so what's the difference? And you're more gone than here anyhow," I told him.

He said I had an answer for everything.

I rooted around the pantry and found an old bag of dog food that I couldn't throw out at the time. I put a couple handfuls on a newspaper and scraped the rest of my grits and ham on top. I knew the minute I fed this cat, we wouldn't get shed of it. Kenny T's words echoed every time I thought about helping out a stray.

When I opened the screen door of the porch, the tabby cat jumped back into the grass but not as far as a wild cat would. Its yellow eyes were big and cautious. Why that little cat didn't know if I'd throw out a scrap or a shoe, but it held its ground, its tail making a nervous sway back and forth.

I dropped the paper of vittles outside the door real quick so not to taint it. That poor skinny thing lunged for that paper before I could get back inside the screen porch. I guess it was ready to take a risk being close to a human to satisfy its hunger.

I eased down in my porch rocker to watch it eat. Its pin teeth gnawed up that ham first with a little growling noise slipping out of its throat. Then it crouched down to crunch those dog pebbles, one at a time. It might have licked that paper clean enough to read again. It yawned, probably feeling satisfied with its full stomach. Its coarse pink tongue gave me a "Meow," then licked up the water in the tray on the bottom of my petunia pot. The creature sat there running its tongue over its paws, transferring a little wet to its face.

I said, "Hey, kitty," a few times, trying to get it not to run off.

Instead, it kept bathing itself, lifting each paw, hardly looking up at me. Then it crept back into the yard, making a wide circle around the edge near the fence, looking back toward me a few times before it loped into taller grass and disappeared behind the shop.

*

The warm sun started streaming in on my shoulders. Must've been dozing when a loud yowl made my head jerk. The stray cat was hanging on the screen door with all fours. That mouth was having its say. "No, no, skedaddle off that door or you'll have it tore to pieces," I hollered and waved my arms. Immediately, guilt slipped in. I was starting to have second thoughts about running it off when the phone jingled.

"Edith, I don't know what I'm going to do?" My friend Ruby's voice sounded urgent.

"You in a mess? I've fed a stray cat, and now we're into it," I said before she could tell me her trouble.

"Who, you and Kenny T? Why, I didn't think he'd want another pet after Watchman."

"That's what he said awhile back. I miss that old dog, too. Kenny T's gone to town. He don't know about this one yet," I sniffed.

"You've fed a cat, right?" Ruby said.

"That's what it looked like." I tried not to give her a tone.

Ruby rattled on, and my mind slipped away. Sometimes I thought I caught a glimpse of the old bird dog still curled up on his favorite recliner in the TV room. The chair used to spring open with the footrest popping out when he leapt off of it too fast. I'd pat the armrest as if his old head was still propped up on it. When I mentioned it to Kenny T, he pulled his wrinkly handkerchief out of his overalls and snorted, but I never told Ruby about that. I just wrote a note to myself in my spiral notebook. I tried to keep track of things I didn't understand.

Ruby said, "Good gracious, he loved that Watchman. Well, I could use a good trapper. I've got mice coming and going around here. I'll come over and take a look at that cat, okay?"

"Uh. . ." The phone clicked in my ear as I was considering. An uneasiness crept into my stomach. I moved back out to the porch and called, "Here, kitty, skeddy, kitty." It crept up out of the grass and rolled itself around right in front of the step. I reached out my hand and almost stroked its dark hair.

*

When I was a girl, my grandmother, Mama Leigh, would not hear of me having a pet. "They carry all manner of disease. And what would you do if it disappeared or died?"

I'd sneak food scraps out to a black feral cat that lived in our barn. It never got close enough for me to touch it. But we had an agreement that I could call it Blackie and sit very still on the loft floor to watch it eat and bathe. I was glad to have someone that asked nothing in return.

One afternoon Mama Leigh climbed the loft ladder and startled us. Blackie got frantic, sailed out of the loft, and tumbled on the barn floor. I watched it limp out the door, still whimpering. Mama Leigh said, "I've saved you from no telling what that cat could spread." I didn't feel saved, just cheated. Each night for a while, I'd slip out my window with a flashlight and take food to the loft, but it piled up. Field mice came instead of Blackie.

Sitting on the porch this morning watching this skeddy cat reminded me I didn't have to listen to Kenny T, but what about Ruby?

She was headstrong. It was hard to hold my own with her sometimes. She probably got that way from school teaching and working in the County Clerk's office. So many people wanted things from her right quick. That husband, Felix, was a trial, fooling around on her for years. I guess we had that in common, but it was hard to talk about. We've been friends for years, better friends after we both retired since she calls everyday. She works me in she'd say with a laugh, still keeping all of her activities on the kitchen calendar. She still goes to yoga class at the Methodist Church and wanders around Orange Hollow center at least once a week. She always finds some project at the house to tend to. I have more time on my hands. My neuropathy slows down my baking and my chores.

*

Ruby's black Ford sent gravel flying from the driveway when she ground her brakes just short of the shop. I waved from the screen porch, then watched her pull out of her trunk a blue box with a handle. She flung open the screen door and plunked down into Kenny T's porch rocker, propping her feet on the blue plastic box. She'd put on her lipstick too fast and barely ran a comb through her fluffy hair. I stared at the box, worrying over that cage-like door, but tried to mask my thoughts with a kind smile. I wished I hadn't lit this fire in her that might get out of control.

Ruby leaned out toward the yard. "Is he out there still?"

"Probably." My chest deflated. Why had I mentioned that cat to her? "It didn't take you long to get over here."

Ruby's plucked eyebrows went up. "Why, it's nearly supper time. You been out here all day?"

When I tried to stand up, the stiffness in my legs made me wince. I'd been losing a little time lately since I'd retired from the school cafeteria, but not this much. My stomach churned a bit. "Want a co-cola?"

"Something stronger'd be better." Ruby laughed. "Get our nerve up to catch this critter."

"You been drinking more of that wine at night," I said, trying to stall her while I considered if I wanted to tap into

Kenny T's stash. I didn't mean to sound accusing. I know being out on the farm without Felix is lonely for her. She'd called me once when she'd had quite a bit.

"I like wine if it's a nice pink," Ruby said evenly, her smeared lips pressed together.

The TV room was cooler than usual when I went in to look behind the couch at Kenny T's bottles. The recliner footrest was sticking out like Watchman had just left it. I patted the armrest and grabbed the first bottle I got my hands on. I slammed the front door that Kenny T must've left open and hurried right on through the pain in my achy legs back to the kitchen.

Ruby was opening cabinet doors looking for glasses. "I only know where the tea glasses are," Ruby said. "You look a little peaked. No lunch?"

I twisted off the cap to the Jack Daniels and poured the strong-smelling liquid over ice cubes in the tea glasses Ruby set out. We both took a sip and coughed.

"I might be crazy, but I swear that dead bird dog has been in Kenny T's recliner."

Ruby took another sip and leaned toward me. "That happen often, Edith?"

I told her about the footrest being sprung open on its own more than once.

Ruby pushed her thin eyebrows together, and her eyes shifted around weirdly like she didn't believe me.

"Did you write any of that in your spiral notebook?" Ruby said.

"What notebook?" I lied, not remembering that I might have told her about my note taking. I shifted my achy legs, but felt a quiet space opening up inside. I glanced toward her, and she was watching me slip back.

Ruby nodded her head like she was greeting a stranger and said real slow, "Okay."

I dropped my eyes and limped toward the porch. We took more sips and eased back into the rockers. She told me she'd seen funny lights in the sky hovering over her house. Then I told her about Blackie, holding its little biscuit head to nuzzle in my hand, and that this twin stray was my second chance to have my own pet.

"Isn't this a tabby?" She turned her head quizzically.

"But it feels like Blackie," is all I could say.

"You've touched it?" Ruby's red mouth stretched into a funny smile.

"In my dreams, silly." I laughed, trying to push her questions away.

"Dreams, hmm. Are you sure there really is a cat, Edith? Maybe it's more like Watchman—you know, ghostly." Ruby's voice was not usually this calm. Her teeth were getting red lipstick on them from moving them around so much against her lips.

She wasn't following what I said, making me wonder, too, if the quiet space was going to swallow me and surround me with confusing ideas. My eyes were feeling drippy, so I squeezed them tight. I let my head fall back onto the rocker headrest. I sniffed. "I'm just going to rock for a minute."

A yowl came from the porch screen. My eyes flashed open. The stray was hanging on the screen door again, then the cat jumped back into the grass when I shrieked, "Did you hear it? It's back."

"Hear what? Where'd it go?" Ruby said, jumping up from Kenny T's rocker. She ran out the screen door clutching the blue box, its open cage door clanging against the side. "Ohhh," she squealed when her foot pushed right through the newspaper covered in mushy grits and dog food.

I shuddered, then sat up straight. "It's over there." I pointed in the opposite direction the cat had run.

About the Author

M aryann Hopper is a writer and storyteller who recorded six of her stories on a CD, *Missing the Magnolias*. She has read her stories at the beginner's tent at the National Storytelling Festival, the National Crone's Counsel, numerous Atlanta venues, and Womonwrites Writing Conference. Recently, she was chosen as a semi-finalist in the Tucson Festival of Books Literary Awards competition and participated in the Master Writers Workshop. She has several short story collections in progress. She lives in Marietta, Georgia, with her partner Drea and their three cats. *Don't Let the Flies In: Edith's Stories* is her first published collection.